DISNEY's

THE LITTLE MERMAID

ARISTA'S NEW BOYFRIEND

DISNEY'S

THE LITTLE MERMAID

ARISTA'S NEW BOYFRIEND

by M. J. Carr

illustrations by Fred Marvin

DISNEY PRESS

NEW YORK

Text and illustrations © 1993 by Disney Press. All rights reserved.
No part of this book may be used or reproduced in any manner
whatsoever without written permission from the publisher. Printed
and bound in the United States of America. For information address
Disney Press, 114 Fifth Avenue, New York, New York 10011.

Library of Congress Catalog Card Number: 92-54511

ISBN: 1-56282-371-X

FIRST EDITION

1 3 5 7 9 10 8 6 4 2

To Jessie Sarah Carr

DISNEY'S

THE LITTLE MERMAID

ARISTA'S NEW BOYFRIEND

Deep in the ocean, in the kingdom of the merpeople, the water was becoming warmer. The seaweed was growing lush and green, and pods of whales were casting their shadows on the royal palace as they migrated overhead. King Triton's daughters knew what all these signs meant. They knew it was the beginning of summer.

Summer was always a special time for the seven mermaid princesses—with no school for two whole months, they were free to do whatever they pleased. But this summer promised to be the most special ever. The King was moving his family and all his court to a brand new summer palace. The princesses had talked of nothing else for weeks. And now, the night before they were to leave, they scurried excitedly about their royal dressing chambers, packing for the trip.

"What shall I bring?" asked Attina.

"Everything!" said Adella.

Attina took a look at the pile of things that Adella was planning on packing. Adella had piled up most of her wardrobe. "We get one trunk each," Attina said. "You're never going to fit all those things into yours. Besides, the dolphin caravan won't be able to pull it all."

"Maybe I'll hitch an extra trunk or two to one of those whales passing overhead," Adella joked.

"Sure," Attina said, laughing, "and have your trunks end up hundreds of miles in the wrong direction!"

Just then King Triton entered the dressing chambers to see how the mermaids were coming along.

"And how are my beautiful daughters?" he asked. "Ready to leave, I hope?"

The King caught sight of the messy piles that cluttered the floor. "Don't forget," he reminded his daughters, "the carriages are coming first thing in the morning."

"I'll never be ready!" shrieked Adella.

"You'd better be," the King said, smiling. "And don't forget your party clothes—your crowns, your jewels. The royal party planner has planned a series of parties for you. Since I will be busy with the affairs of state for most of the summer, I've asked her to keep you as busy as possible. There'll also be shows to see, tournaments to play in, and, naturally, a dinner or two in your honor. There'll be festivities nearly every night of the week."

King Triton needn't have reminded his daughters about their party outfits. They'd all remembered to set those aside. Their father had told them often enough that this would be the most glittering social season they'd ever had. Many other important families were joining them at the summer

palace—dukes and duchesses, lords and ladies.

"You'll be meeting many families who live in the area of our summer palace," Triton said once more. "And many of them have children about your age. It's always good to meet more girls and boys, and the parties will be just the place to do so!"

The King smiled at each of his daughters, then turned and swam back to his royal chambers. He had many things to attend to before morning.

"Boys," sighed Aquata after her father had left the room. "I hope I meet the son of a duke."

"I hope I meet the son of an earl," said Andrina.

"I hope I meet them *all*," laughed Adella.

The mermaids turned their attention back to packing. Of the seven sisters, only one was definitely not excited about moving to the summer palace and meeting merboys. Arista wanted to stay right where she was. She wanted to stay near the palace stables and the sea horses she loved to ride. She had been looking forward to going riding all summer long.

The King had already assured Arista that there'd be stables for her at the new palace, too. But it wouldn't be the same, Arista thought. At the royal stables, she knew all the sea horses by name. And she knew how to ride each one. She knew, for instance, which one liked to go fast and which one swam best through a stormy ocean when the waters were rolling and sand was churned up.

"Don't you think it's going to be even a *little* sad leaving?" Arista asked her sisters, looking at each one in turn. "Aren't any of you going to miss anything here?"

Alana stopped a moment to consider. "I'll miss my gardens," she said.

"I'll miss my library," Attina chimed in.

Ariel didn't say anything. She knew what she would miss, but she couldn't tell her sisters. She'd miss the grotto where she kept all the human treasures she'd collected. She had to keep the grotto a secret, though. It was forbidden to collect anything having to do with humans.

One by one the mermaids finished packing and went off to bed. Arista slipped out of the palace to visit the royal stables one last time. She put her arms around each of the sea horses and said good-bye.

"I'll miss you," she said to Foamy, who was her favorite. "I'm sure the sea horses at the new palace won't be anywhere near as sleek or as swift."

She gave Foamy one last hug and went back to the palace. It would be a long summer. Of *that,* Arista was sure.

"Oh!" gasped Ariel as her carriage pulled up to the new palace. "I've never seen anything like it!"

The summer palace was indeed beautiful. The princesses slipped out of their carriages and stared up at the gleaming coral turrets.

"And wait till you see the ballroom," said their father. He led his daughters through a vast pearl-studded hall and into the large, open ballroom. There the walls were covered with beautiful mosaics made of small pieces of brightly colored shells. "This is where our parties will be," the King said.

Aquata bowed low, pretending she was a merboy at a party. "Would m'lady care to dance?" she asked Attina.

"But of course," Attina replied in her most ladylike voice. She giggled. This summer was going to be fun!

The sisters swam off excitedly to their suite of rooms to unpack and get settled. They had to hurry. A party to commemorate the start of summer was planned for that very evening.

"What shall I wear?" asked Adella. "My pearl tiara or the one made of periwinkle?"

"Where's my coral necklace?" cried Alana, rifling through her trunk. "I can't go to the party without my coral necklace!"

While her sisters were bustling about, Arista stared out the window at the different fish gliding by. She was thinking of her sea horses; she was thinking that she wouldn't have to worry about tiaras or jewels at all if she were at home, riding.

Around her, her sisters were getting more and more giddy.

"How many boys do you think will be there?" asked Alana.

"A hundred!" answered Aquata.

"Really?"

"Well," Aquata said sheepishly, "at least ten."

Andrina started dancing around the others, unable to contain her excitement. "I'm going to meet the boy of my dreams," she said, twirling around and around.

The excitement was contagious. All the sisters, with the exception of Arista, began to laugh and talk at once.

Ariel noticed how quiet Arista was being.

"Is something the matter?" Ariel asked her sister. "Why aren't you dressed? Didn't you bring your party clothes?"

"I don't want to go to the party," Arista said quietly, but not quietly enough. At once, all her sisters were swimming around her in disbelief.

"You don't want to go to the party?" said Andrina. "Why not? Sebastian says the band he put together is great! Surely you won't want to miss all the dancing."

"Or the boys," Adella reminded her.

"I don't care about the boys," said Arista.

"Maybe you do care about them," suggested Ariel. "Maybe you're just shy."

"Shy!" cried Arista indignantly. "Me, shy? I don't think so." She wished her sisters would just leave her alone.

"Maybe you're scared because you don't know them yet," Ariel persisted. "They're not the boys we're used to."

"Once and for all," Arista said sharply, "I'm not scared of boys. I have plenty of boyfriends back home. Why should I be scared of any boys at the party? I bet I could outride each and every one who shows up!"

"Oh, so that's what this is about," said Andrina. "It's about sea horses." The sisters giggled.

"Maybe it's easier to talk to sea horses than to boys," Adella teased.

Arista looked at her sisters crowding around her, laughing. She didn't want to talk to *them* anymore. "Cut it out," she said.

Andrina put her arms around the neck of an imaginary sea horse. "Oh, Foamy," she said, batting her eyelashes, "I love you so much."

Arista glared at Andrina. She pushed past her sisters and swam out the door, leaving a thick stream of bubbles in her wake.

"That wasn't very nice," Ariel said to Andrina.

"Oh, she'll come back," said Aquata. "She knows we're just teasing."

Outside the palace Arista swam angrily toward the stables. "Easier to talk to sea horses," she muttered. "Well, maybe it *is*. Better than talking to some stupid son of a duke or a count. I can't believe they think I'm afraid of boys. As if I'd ever be afraid of a *boy*."

Arista could see the new stables in the distance. "I'll just go in and look at the sea horses," she said to herself. "They won't be *my* sea horses, but at least they'll be better than those giggling sisters of mine."

As Arista swam closer, she could just make out the sea horses' heads through the stables' open doors.

Suddenly she stopped. From out of nowhere, it seemed, a merboy appeared riding bareback on a sea horse. He was the most beautiful merboy Arista had ever seen—

and so skillful and swift a rider! Arista found herself unable to move.

The merboy's dark hair streamed out in the water behind him as he reined in the sea horse and dismounted. He was totally unaware of Arista, who was still several yards away. He unsaddled the steed and began grooming him.

"Good work, Current," Arista heard him say. "You've really earned your oats and plankton today."

Arista slipped behind a tall patch of plants and watched as the merboy groomed his sea horse. It occurred to her that maybe she *was* feeling a little shy after all—though this was the first boy who'd ever made her feel that way.

She stayed hidden for a while longer, but pretty soon the plants began to sway in the choppy evening waters, and Arista knew it was time to head back to the palace. Her sisters would come looking for her if she was gone too long, and she certainly didn't want them coming *here*. This gorgeous merboy was one new discovery she wanted to keep all to herself!

When Arista got back to the palace, she had just enough time to get dressed for the party.

"Hurry," Ariel urged. "We're all ready."

"Though we've all changed our outfits at least once," admitted Alana.

"I think Adella's changed hers five times by now," Ariel said, laughing.

"What do you think?" Adella asked uncertainly, examining her periwinkle tiara in the mirror. "Should I put the pearl tiara back on?"

"NO!" her sisters exclaimed in unison.

Arista chose a simple mother-of-pearl necklace from her own box of jewels, clasped it around her neck, and swam up to join her sisters.

"Hey, Arista," said Andrina. "It looks as though you're in a better mood."

"Hmmm . . . ?" Arista asked dreamily.

"She may be in a better mood," said Aquata, "but it looks like she's not exactly here. Hello," Aquata called out, waving her hand in front of Arista's face. "Hello, Arista. Are you there?"

"She's thinking of her sea horses," said Andrina. "You know that dreamy look she always gets when she's thinking about her sea horses."

"Arista," Adella said firmly. "Don't think sea horses. Think boys. Repeat after me. Boys."

"Boy," said Arista. She had just one very specific merboy in mind.

Together the princesses swam off to the ballroom, with Arista trailing a bit behind. They stopped when they reached the entrance. The ballroom was filled with guests, all gaily attired. At the far end of the room sat King Triton, on a shell-encrusted throne. Beside him was the new band, with Sebastian at the conductor's podium. Even Sebastian was smartly dressed. He wore a black bow tie around his neck and held a shiny new crystal baton.

A small blue fish swam up to the entrance to announce the mermaids. "The royal princesses!" he said loudly, and then called out each of their names. As soon as he finished, the band struck up a number, and a group of merboys swam up to ask the princesses to dance. The merboys whisked the mermaids onto the dance floor and spun them around in a whirl.

Arista found herself dancing with Corporal Carp's son, Randolph, who went to military school. Randolph wore epaulets on a jacket covered with medals and had a sheathed sword strapped to his side. He was not a very good dancer. Each time he spun Arista around, the sword banged into her.

"Lovely night," he said, trying to make small talk.

"Yes it is," said Arista. She was actually

thinking it might be the loveliest night of her life.

"The current is so mild," Randolph continued.

"Current . . ." Arista thought of the beautiful steed she had seen the merboy riding at the stables. "Yes, he is a beautiful sea horse," she said.

"Sea horse?" asked Randolph. "I thought we were talking about the current." He looked confused.

"Yes, of course. You're right. Current," Arista said quickly.

Randolph looked at her curiously. "So you're one of King Triton's daughters," he went on.

"That's right. I'm Arista," she told him.

"Princess Arista. You know, most of the guests here tonight are titled as well." Arista did not look impressed, but Randolph went on anyway. "That boy there, for instance, is the son of the Duke of Whales. And that boy you see dancing next to us is a descendant of an earl of the China Sea. As for myself, well, my father is the courageous Corporal Carp, who single-handedly defeated the . . ."

Arista smiled and nodded, pretending to be interested. But this Randolph Carp was definitely too impressed with himself for her taste.

When the music stopped, Arista was finally able to excuse herself, but seconds later she was caught up by yet another eager merboy. Over the course of the night, Arista danced with many merboys, but she couldn't remember any of their names, nor did she want to. She thought a lot of them were stuck-up and boring.

One merboy talked her ear off, bragging about all the trophies he'd won at a variety of sporting events.

Arista thought for a moment. "Did you ever win a trophy in sea horse racing?" she asked, hopeful that if the young merman shared an interest in riding, they would at least have *something* in common.

"Oh, heavens no," laughed the merboy. "Mother and Father would never permit us to *race* sea horses. But I do play a mean game of polo!"

Another merboy talked on and on about his collection of tropical plants, but Arista couldn't keep her mind on what he was saying. She was completely lost in her thoughts. And she certainly couldn't tell any of these merboys what she was thinking about—a merboy, outside the palace, at the stables, who had a sure hand with the sea horses and a love of riding like Arista herself.

Arista looked around. Her sisters seemed to be having such a good time. When she danced by Aquata, Aquata was laughing loudly at a joke her dancing partner had just told her.

I danced with that boy, thought Arista. I didn't think his jokes were funny.

When she danced by Ariel, her younger sister was talking animatedly to another of the merboys. "That's exactly how *I* feel," Ariel was saying brightly. "We seem to agree on so many things."

When the song ended, Arista excused herself from her partner and floated off by herself to a corner of the room. She watched the party as if it were a show on a stage and she were in the audience. Merfolk were laughing, dancing, talking, and eating. They all really seem to like this sort of thing, she thought.

Arista wished she could leave the party and go back to the stables. She thought about how nervous and shy she'd been before and how she couldn't even bring herself to say hi to the merboy she had seen there. Maybe her sisters were right. Maybe she *was* afraid of boys.

Just then another merboy from the party swam up and asked her to dance, interrupting her thoughts. "No thank you," Arista answered politely.

"Are you sure?" he asked, a little surprised at the rejection.

"I think I need a rest," Arista told him.

The merboy bowed and swam away. Arista looked around. No one was watching her. She edged toward the door of the ballroom. The band finished its song. When all the merfolk turned to applaud Sebastian and his musicians, Arista slipped unnoticed out the door.

As Arista swam toward the stables, she began to worry that the merboy she had seen earlier might now be gone. Arista swam closer. There he was! Arista paused by the same grouping of plants she had hid behind earlier. She had to gather her courage.

She watched the merboy move from one sea horse to the next as he groomed them. What if he didn't want to talk to her? she worried. What if she said the wrong thing?

Arista knew that no matter what might

happen, she just had to take the chance. She swam up to the stables and through the doorway.

"Hello," she said quickly. The merboy turned to look at her, surprised. Arista stuck out her hand rather awkwardly. "My name is Arista," she said. "Who are you?"

"Dylan," said the merboy.

Arista stopped. Now what? She hadn't really thought past introducing herself, and she wasn't sure what else to say. "You like sea horses?" she asked abruptly.

"Love them," said Dylan. "I can't think of anything in this ocean I like more."

"Me, too!" Arista blurted out. "Actually," she said, "I knew you liked sea horses. I could tell by the way you were riding when I saw you before. I never saw anyone ride a sea horse as well as you do."

"You were watching me?" asked Dylan.

Arista blushed. "Well, I couldn't help but see you," she tried to explain. "I was here a few hours ago checking out the stables my father had built for me, and . . ."

"Your father?" Dylan interrupted. "You mean you're one of King Triton's daughters?"

23

"Arista." Arista held her hand out awkwardly again. "Oh," she said, pulling it back. "I guess I already said that."

"You're one of the princesses?" Dylan asked.

"That's right," said Arista. She hoped her being a princess didn't make Dylan nervous. Sometimes merpeople acted differently around her when they found out who she was.

Arista cleared her throat. "What about you?" she asked. "Why are you out here at the stables tonight?"

"I work here," said Dylan. "My parents are grounds keepers at the palace. I was hired for the summer to muck out the stalls." He wiped his hands on a rag. "I'm the stableboy."

"Hey, that's great," Arista said, impressed. "It must be fun to take care of sea horses all day—and get paid for it, too!"

Dylan laughed. "Yeah, I guess." He looked at Arista's mother-of-pearl necklace. "So, why aren't you over at the palace for the big festivities?" he asked.

"Because I wanted to meet you," Arista

said, surprised at the words that were coming out of her mouth. She couldn't believe she'd said that!

"Really?" Dylan asked, grinning.

"Really," said Arista. "And, of course, I wanted to meet all the sea horses, too," she added quickly. "Current, for instance. Will you introduce me?"

"Well, of course I will, Your Highness. Or . . . Your Princessness—" Dylan stopped short. "What should I call you?"

"Arista," she laughed.

Dylan introduced Arista to all the sea horses in the stables. "Current's the wildest," he said. "When I first met him, he'd sooner buck me than carry me, but now we've got an understanding, don't we, boy?" Dylan patted Current on the nose.

"Is he really that wild?" asked Arista.

"I'll tell you what," said Dylan. He gestured toward another strong stallion who was bucking in the next stall. "You ride Tide there," he said, "and see if you can keep up." Dylan saddled the sea horses and slid up onto Current. Arista mounted Tide.

"Keep up?" Arista said when she was settled. "That'll be no problem! Come on! Let's go!"

The sea horses sped through the cool night ocean. Water streamed across Arista's cheeks as she urged Tide on. Arista and Dylan rode away from the palace, away from the part of the ocean settled by merfolk, and into a part where there were fish that Arista had never even seen before.

"What's that beautiful striped one?" she asked. "And that pretty blue-green one over there?"

Dylan told Arista everything he knew about the sea life in the waters that surrounded the palace. He showed her all the sights he could think to show. "Of course, we have to be careful out here," he said. "There are plenty of dangerous fish, not just pretty ones."

"Dangerous?" asked Arista. "Like what?"

"Like sharks, for instance. Or barracuda. I've seen electric eels around here, and a man-of-war. Once I saw a devilfish. Have you ever seen a devilfish?"

"I don't think so."

"They're huge," explained Dylan. "And deadly."

Arista looked around at the unfamiliar ocean that surrounded her. She knew that she ought to be getting back to the palace. "Do you think we've been gone a long time?" she asked.

"We can head back if you want," said Dylan. "But first, how'd you like to learn a little trick or two?"

"Sure!" said Arista.

"Watch this," said Dylan. Dylan hopped up onto Current's back and balanced on his tail. He nodded to Arista to try it, too. Arista balanced carefully on Tide's back as Dylan reached over to help hold her steady.

Arista grinned broadly. She couldn't believe her luck. Not only had she met a merboy who loved sea horses as much as she did, but she'd met one who could teach her a thing or two.

"Fun, huh?" Dylan said.

"Fun!" Arista agreed.

The two slid back down into their saddles, then rode back to the palace. When they got there, Arista could see that the party had just ended. Merfolk were spilling out of the ballroom and into carriages that were waiting at the palace gate.

"Wait!" Arista whispered to Dylan. "Over there." She directed him behind a reef so that none of the merfolk coming from the party would see them. Randolph Carp, the merboy from military school, passed right in front of them.

"It's all a matter of breeding," she heard him say loudly. "The better people are always from better families."

Dylan looked at Arista. "Why are we hiding?" he whispered. "Are you ashamed of me?"

"No!" Arista said quickly. "It's just that I was supposed to *be* at this party, remember?" She grinned at Dylan, then turned back to watch the extravagantly dressed merfolk.

"Uh, I'd better go now," Arista said. "Can I see you tomorrow?"

"You know where to find me," said Dylan.

"Great," said Arista. "Thanks for everything. I had a terrific time."

And with that, she slid off her sea horse and handed the reins to Dylan. Then Arista swam quickly back to the palace to join her sisters, who were headed back to their bedroom suite, in high spirits from the glitter and excitement of the ball.

The next morning, when the mermaid princesses gathered for breakfast, there was one topic of conversation and one only—merboys.

"Did you talk to the boy with the sword strapped around his waist?" asked Alana.

"*Talk* to him?" said Andrina. "Did you *dance* with him? That sword of his kept banging into me the whole time."

"Yes, but what about that handsome one whose father is a count?" Attina asked.

Now all the sisters began to join in. "You mean Shelldon? The tall, cute blond one who goes to private school in the Mediterranean?" asked Aquata.

"That's the one."

"Hey," Adella cut in, "don't get any ideas. He's the one *I* like."

"*You* like? I was talking to him for at least half an hour," Aquata argued.

"Well, that may be," said Adella. "But he asked me to dance five times. Or was it six. . . ."

Aquata threw a small pebble at Adella, and Adella lobbed it playfully back.

"What about you, Arista?" asked Ariel. "Did you have a good time last night? Did you meet anyone special?"

Arista thought for a moment. She wasn't sure she should tell her sisters about Dylan. But since everyone was in such a good mood this morning, she decided to go ahead. "As a matter of fact," she started to say.

But Arista never got to finish her sentence, for right at that moment King Triton swam in and took his place at the head of the table. "So," he said with a twinkle in his eye.

"I trust you all had a good time at the party last night?"

"Yes!" the sisters chorused.

"It certainly looked as if you were having a good time. At least from where I sat." The King sighed contentedly. "It was such a delight to watch my beautiful daughters mingling with the children of some of my best friends. Nothing would make me happier than to see you become friends with young people from such fine, upstanding families, families I know as well as I know my own."

Arista looked down at her plate. The things her father was saying were upsetting her. All the qualities he seemed to think were important in a merboy were ones that had nothing to do with Dylan or his family. Dylan's parents worked as grounds keepers. She wasn't sure her father would like that.

"Well," King Triton said as he raised himself from the table. "I'm off to attend to the business of the kingdom. You girls have a good time."

The mermaids smiled sweetly at their father until he left the room. Then they immediately turned back to each other.

"So," said Aquata. "Where were we? I know we were discussing something important."

"We were discussing Arista," said Ariel. "I asked her if she met anyone last night."

"Right," said Aquata. She turned to Arista. "And you started to say, 'As a matter of fact . . .' "

All the mermaids looked expectantly at Arista, waiting to hear what she had to say. Arista pushed her breakfast around on her plate.

"Well," she said, "what I started to say was, as a matter of fact, I *didn't* meet anyone special."

"Oh," said Aquata. She was disappointed. Her other sisters were disappointed, too, but just for a moment. Then they went back to talking about the party. Only Ariel paused to look at Arista. She suspected that something was not quite right. As a matter of fact, Ariel didn't remember seeing her sister at all the night before.

After the mermaids finished their breakfast, they started to talk about how they were going to spend their first full day of summer vacation. Alana said she was going to go fish-watching to find out what particular creatures lived in this region of the ocean. Attina announced that she was going to curl up with a good book.

"What are you going to do, Ariel?" Andrina asked.

Ariel was planning to search for human treasures, but she couldn't tell that to her sisters. "I'm not sure," she said. "Maybe I'll just take a nice long swim."

"And what about you, Arista?"

"I'm off to the stables," Arista said with a smile.

"Naturally," said Adella. "If you can't find a boy you like, you might as well cozy up to a sea horse," she teased.

Arista was tempted right then to tell her sisters everything, but she stopped herself. After what her father had said, she thought that maybe it wasn't the right time. And anyway, she enjoyed having a secret to keep to herself.

Before anyone could say another word, Arista got up from the table and swam off in the direction of the stables.

* * *

At the stables, Dylan was busy "mucking out," as he called it. When Arista swam in, he looked up with an impish smile, and a lone black curl fell down onto his forehead. "Hey there," he said happily.

Dylan and Arista spent the whole day riding on Current and Tide. Dylan taught Arista how to mount a sea horse while the sea horse was moving. And he taught her how to somersault from one sea horse to another. He also showed her how to ride faster than she ever thought she could ride.

Later in the day, while riding with Dylan through the ocean, Arista spotted Ariel in the distance. "This way," Arista quickly called to Dylan. She didn't want her sister to see him.

On their way back to the palace, Arista spied Alana feeding some striped fish. "Come on," she beckoned to Dylan again, this time hurrying them out of Alana's sight.

When they got back to the stables, Dylan slid off his horse, then helped Arista off hers.

"Those girls are your sisters, aren't they?"

he asked. "Why didn't you want them to see me? Are you afraid they won't approve of me?"

"No, it's not that," Arista said.

"Well, what is it then?" Dylan persisted.

Arista looked into the eyes of her new friend. How could she possibly tell Dylan that she *was* afraid that her father would never approve of him? Arista just couldn't tell Dylan that.

"I'll introduce you to my family," she said instead. "But I'm not ready to just yet. Maybe next week," she offered.

Dylan watched Arista's face closely.

"No, really," she said. "Next week you'll meet my sisters."

"And your father?" he asked.

"Oh, sure, and my father, too." But Arista knew that she was only kidding herself—and that she had just lied to Dylan.

Each of the mermaid sisters, in her own
way, was enjoying the summer as the days
passed.

Ariel spent her free time swimming in the
warm waters, hunting for human treasures.
Attina was reading almost a book a day, and
Alana was discovering all sorts of new
creatures. Adella, Andrina, and Aquata spent
most of their days talking about the merboys
they'd met. And Arista found herself spending
more and more time with Dylan. Arista, in

fact, was spending so much time away from the palace that her sisters had begun to notice.

"Where's Arista always disappearing to?" asked Attina.

"The stables, I guess," said Alana. "But she's been acting strangely, hasn't she?"

"How much time can she spend with those sea horses of hers?" asked Andrina.

"If she doesn't watch out, she's going to start eating oats and plankton," Adella joked.

Not only did Arista spend many of her days with Dylan, but almost every evening, too. Instead of attending the various parties and activities held for the princesses at the palace, Arista would arrive along with her sisters, greet her father like a dutiful daughter, and then, when she thought she wouldn't be missed, sneak out and race over to the stables.

Sometimes, as she was getting ready for the parties, Arista wondered if she should just forget all her fears and bring Dylan along. I could just show up with him one night, she thought. I could swim right up to Father's throne and introduce them. "Father, this is Dylan, my new boyfriend," I could say. "I met him in the stables, where he works. And Dylan, this is King Triton, ruler of all the oceans."

Somehow Arista could never imagine it turning out quite right. She pictured her father's face looming in front of her, stern and angry. "Who are his parents?" she imagined her father saying. "Do I know them?"

As the days wore on, Dylan would still ask Arista, once in a while, when she was going to introduce him to her family. But even though she kept saying it would be soon, Dylan sensed she just was not ready to. He stopped asking and tried very hard not to be hurt. Instead, the two friends spent their time together doing what they both loved best—riding sea horses.

Some days Dylan taught Arista how to perform stunts, and other days they rode far away from the palace, where the ocean stretched out for leagues and leagues in front of them. There they would race each other, and each day Arista found herself riding faster. Dylan had not only become her best friend, he'd become her coach as well.

*   *   *

One day Dylan and Arista rode so far away from the palace that Arista didn't think she'd need to be on the lookout for her sisters. She didn't notice Ariel, who was busily scanning the ocean floor just a short distance away.

Ariel didn't see her older sister right away, either. She had just found the most remarkable human treasure. It was round and shiny, and it was attached to a beautiful gold chain. At first Ariel thought it was some strange sort of clam, but upon closer inspection she could see that it was much, much prettier than a clam. It had numbers all along one side of it and three long thin pieces in the center—one of which was moving!

Ariel was holding the treasure very close to her face when suddenly she heard a ticking noise. "I wonder what this could be," she said, turning the object around in her hands.

Ariel then spotted Arista. She quickly hid the forbidden treasure in her satchel.

41

"Arista!" Ariel called out. She hadn't caught sight of Dylan yet. "Arista!"

Arista reined in her steed and looked to see who was calling her. Dylan rode into Ariel's view. "Oh no!" groaned Arista as she watched Ariel swim toward them.

"You two certainly were riding fast," Ariel started chattering. "I wasn't even sure that you heard me. Arista, I don't think I've ever seen you ride that fast." Ariel looked at Dylan and smiled a friendly smile. She waited for Arista to introduce them. Arista didn't. "Who's your friend?" Ariel asked brightly.

"This is Dylan," said Arista. "Dylan, this is my youngest sister, Ariel."

"Pleased to meet you," Dylan said.

"You sure can ride!" Ariel was impressed.

"Dylan's taught me a lot since I came here," said Arista. "I owe everything I've learned to him."

Ariel looked at Arista. Then she looked at Dylan. She looked back at Arista, and suddenly it all made sense.

"Oh, I get it," she said, putting the story together in her head. "So *that's* where you've been spending all your time. You haven't been alone with the sea horses, you've been riding with Dylan."

"That's right," said Arista.

"But why have you been so secretive?"

Dylan looked at Arista. He wanted to know the answer to that question, too. Arista knew she'd have to explain.

"Because of Father," she finally admitted. "All his talk about the aristocratic families he knows and how he wants us to spend time with young people from families he's known practically his whole life. I met Dylan because he works at the stables," she explained proudly, though her voice was shaking a little. "I just didn't think Father would approve of him."

"Did you ever ask Father?" Ariel questioned.

"Oh, you know Father," Arista sighed. "He's so strict and protective. He has such set ideas about what he thinks we should and shouldn't do."

Ariel knew that was true. She clutched her satchel, thinking of the human treasure she'd hidden inside. She knew her father would be furious if he ever found out about all the treasures she'd collected. Still, she didn't entirely agree with Arista. Their father might be strict and protective, but he could also be very understanding. "Arista, maybe if you—" she started to say.

"Forget it," Arista interrupted. "Ariel," she said, looking at her sister pleadingly, "you've got to promise me that you'll never say a word about Dylan to anyone. Don't tell Father, don't tell Adella, don't tell Alana, don't tell *anyone*. You promise?"

Ariel bit her lip. "But . . . "

"Say it," Arista insisted.

"Oh, OK. I promise." Ariel figured she'd just as well stay out of it.

"Maybe we should get back to the palace," said Arista. "Come on. I'll give you a ride," she said, and she helped Ariel onto her sea horse.

The three rode back in silence. Arista knew that Dylan was disappointed in her. She was afraid to look him in the eye. She dropped Ariel off close to the palace, and then she and Dylan took the sea horses back to the stables.

"I'm sorry," she said as she unhitched her saddle.

"That's OK. I understand," Dylan said with a shrug. "You're a princess. I'm a stableboy." Arista noticed the hurt look in his eyes.

Arista sighed. She wished that Dylan were a duke's son. That would make everything so much easier. Of course, then he wouldn't be Dylan, she thought. Well, then she wished that she could have been born a regular person instead of a princess. But in her heart Arista knew that that was not the answer, either.

What Arista really wished was that she could have the courage to tell her father about Dylan—and be brave enough to stand up to whatever it was her father might say. And suddenly Arista knew exactly what she had to do.

Arista paused in front of her father's chambers and thought over what she was going to say. "Father," she would say, "I've become friends with the boy who works at the stables. I really like him. Can I invite him to a party?" Arista took a deep breath and knocked on the door.

"Arista!" King Triton said, surprised. "I was just thinking about you."

"You were?" said Arista.

"Indeed I was. I need some help, and I've

decided that you would be the daughter best suited to the task. I thought of you for this," he said, "because, frankly, you don't seem to be having a good time at our social events."

Arista thought she saw her chance to tell her father what she was really doing. "Father, I've been—"

"Don't interrupt, Arista," said Triton.

"Yes, Father."

"So," the King continued, "I've just received a message from my dear old friend the Earl of Estuary saying that he and his son are arriving for this evening's festivities. He's specifically requested that his son escort one of my daughters to the affair."

Arista's heart sank. "But Father . . ."

"No buts, Arista. I think you'll like the boy. His name is Eddy, and his father tells me he's an expert in courtly diction."

Arista stared at her father. "Father, I don't think I can do this," she said weakly. She no longer felt able to say what she'd come to say.

"Nonsense," her father said. "Of course you can."

"But I . . . ," Arista began.

"Arista, it's all been arranged," the King said. "Now go get ready for the party."

"Yes, Father," Arista replied wearily.

Outside the King's chambers Arista broke down in tears. Why did everything have to be so complicated? she wondered. She'd tried to do the right thing, and now the situation was worse than it had been before. Now she had to spend the whole evening with some *other* merboy. She didn't want to entertain another boy. She wanted to be with Dylan.

Still, Arista knew she had to do what her father asked.

"It will be like baby-sitting," she muttered angrily. "Baby-sitting some stupid boy who's old enough to take care of himself!"

That night, when the party started, Arista arrived with her sisters, and the King immediately introduced her to Eddy, the Earl's son. As the band struck up the first song, Eddy invited Arista to dance.

"I suppose you're looking forward to an introduction to my father, the Earl," Eddy said to Arista as he danced her awkwardly around. Arista was not, of course, looking forward to any such thing. "Well, Father's been detained a bit," Eddy chatted on, "though he's quite anxious to meet you. Sporting fellow, my father. I take after him, I'm proud to say. Chip off the old block and all."

Arista didn't like the airs this merboy put on when he talked. She was definitely not looking forward to spending an entire evening with him.

"Father's assured me that you and I ought to get on famously," said Eddy enthusiastically. He spun Arista around, and she collided into another couple. Arista smiled wanly. She wanted to leave. She really wanted to see Dylan. Earlier she'd gone over to the stables to tell him she wouldn't be by that evening. He looked sad, then jealous when she'd told him about Eddy.

Just then the music stopped, and everyone turned to applaud Sebastian's band.

"Would you excuse me for a moment?" Arista said to Eddy.

"Excuse you?" he asked, puzzled.

"I must go check on something," she said

vaguely. And with that, Arista swam away and out the door.

Eddy waited patiently for Arista to return. The band played another song and then another. Meanwhile, Eddy's father had arrived and found his son alone by the dance floor.

"Where's the young princess?" he asked.

Eddy just shrugged. "I thought she'd be back by now," he said.

A few songs later, when Arista still hadn't returned, Eddy and his father swam around the ballroom looking for her. But Arista was nowhere to be found. They realized it was time to call the matter to King Triton's attention.

"Gone?" cried the King. "What do you mean Arista's gone?"

Ariel, who had been dancing near the King's throne, heard her father shouting.

"Arista probably just stepped out for a moment," Ariel said, trying to cover for her sister.

"Stepped out?" said the King. "Eddy tells me she's been gone for quite a while. She may be in some sort of trouble. We must organize a search party at once!"

"Father, there's really no need for that," Ariel said quickly. She had a feeling she knew where Arista was. "I'll go look for her."

"Nonsense," said the King. "I won't have you out at night all by yourself." The King called to his guards.

"Then let me go with you," said Ariel. She had a plan. Once the search party left the palace, she'd break away and try to find Ariel and Dylan on her own. Then she could warn them that King Triton was on his way!

8

Not far from the palace and the party, Dylan and Arista were riding their sea horses, unaware of what was happening.

"Look," said Dylan. "A devilfish!" A short distance away a very large devilfish was skimming the ocean floor. "Come quick. We'll hide in this cove. Maybe it won't see us."

"I didn't think they were so big!" whispered Arista.

"I told you they were big."

"It looks dangerous."

"It is," Dylan said. "But don't worry. It can't see us. We're safe in here."

The devilfish hovered near them, then glided away. Dylan motioned to Arista. "Come on," he said. "Now's our chance to get out of here. If the devilfish is going that way, we'll go in the opposite direction."

Arista quietly followed Dylan out of the cove.

"I wouldn't want to tangle with that thing," she said, looking back.

"Neither would I," said Dylan. "Let's get out of here."

Arista and Dylan rode their sea horses away from the cove and into the open. They didn't even notice King Triton and the search party coming toward them.

"Who goes there?" King Triton called.

"Oh no!" whispered Arista. "It's my father!" She looked around. There was no place to hide.

"I say, who goes there?" King Triton called again. "Is that you, Arista?"

Arista had no other choice—she had to answer. "Yes, Father!" she called back.

"Arista!" King Triton looked angry—*very* angry. "Where have you been? What are you doing out here in the depths of the ocean at night?" Then King Triton spotted Dylan. "Who are you?" he demanded.

"Father, this is my friend Dylan," Arista said, just as she had rehearsed many times.

King Triton looked suspiciously from the merboy to his daughter and then back to the merboy again. "Why did you leave the party?" he asked Arista sternly.

"Because I didn't want to stay," Arista said miserably. Her voice was shaking. "Father, I've been trying to explain something to you, but you wouldn't listen."

"Explain something to me? Explain what?"

Arista took a deep breath, trying to muster up the courage to continue. "I've been trying to tell you that I have a new friend—Dylan. I didn't want to stay at the party because I didn't want to dance with some other boy. I wanted to be with Dylan. And if I couldn't do that, then I didn't want to be there at all."

The King's face reddened with anger. "So this is *your* fault," he accused Dylan.

"No, sire," Dylan sputtered. "I . . ."

"Well, who are you exactly, anyway?" the King cut him off.

"You haven't met me, Your Majesty," said Dylan. His whole body was shaking, and his voice was, too. "I met Arista at the stables when she came to ride. I'm the stableboy, sire. I take care of the sea horses."

Before Triton could respond to this bit of news, the group was joined by Eddy and his father.

"Ah, Triton," said the Earl. "We thought we'd lost you. I see you've found your daughter."

"Arista," the King said, glaring at his daughter, "this is my dear friend the Earl of Estuary. He and Eddy traveled a full day to get here." Triton turned to the Earl.

"Excuse me for a moment, my friend," he said. "I have something I want to say to my daughter in private." The King took Arista by the arm, and they swam off to the side. A very worried Dylan swam discreetly behind them.

"Do you see the embarrassing situation you've put me in?" the King thundered.

Arista hung her head. "I'll expect *you* to explain everything to the Earl."

"*Me?*" said Arista.

"Yes. You're the one who was so rude to his son."

"Father, I just . . ."

"Arista, I don't want to hear another word. You promised me you'd be at the party tonight, and it appears you deliberately chose to disobey me. You've disappointed the Earl and his son. And you've worried everyone at the party. When you didn't return, we all thought you might be in trouble. Why, Ariel was so concerned that she insisted on joining the search party."

"Ariel?" Arista asked. She looked around. Ariel was nowhere in sight.

"She was here a moment ago," the King said. He scanned the group that accompanied him. "I know I saw her when we passed by the cove."

"The cove!" Arista cried. "Which cove?"

The King pointed in the direction Arista and Dylan had come from. "That cove over there."

"Oh no!" Arista cried.

"The devilfish!" cried Dylan.

Dylan swam swiftly toward Current and took off as fast as he could. Arista hopped on Tide and rode after Dylan. King Triton and the search party followed as quickly as they could.

Ariel was in danger! There was no time to lose!

Dylan sped toward the cove. As he drew
near, he could see the large, dark shape of
the devilfish hovering near a craggy wall of
the cove. Arista rode up beside him.

"Do you see anything?" she asked.

"There it is," Dylan said quietly, pointing
toward the wall.

Arista squinted. "Why do you think it's
hugging the wall like that?"

"Looks as if it's got something trapped in
the cove," Dylan said nervously.

"Ariel!" Arista cried.

Dylan urged his sea horse on. Thinking quickly, he came up with a plan. "I'll distract the devilfish," he called over his shoulder to Arista. "When it turns its attention to me, go in as fast as you can. Grab Ariel and get her out of there!"

With that, Dylan charged at the devilfish. The devilfish, surprised, turned away from the wall, revealing Ariel. She had indeed been trapped in the cove.

"Go!" Dylan shouted to Arista.

Arista took a deep breath, then rode past Dylan and the large, looming devilfish and held out her arm to Ariel. "Grab hold!" she yelled. "Now!" When Ariel grabbed her hand, Arista hoisted her sister onto the back of the sea horse and rode her quickly to safety.

King Triton and the search party swam up just in time to see Arista's brave feat. But then they noticed that the devilfish had cornered Dylan and Current.

"It will sting the boy!" King Triton cried. "The tail of the devilfish is deadly!"

Arista rode up to the search party and

dropped off Ariel. "Keep back!" she said. "All of you!" She sped toward the devilfish in order to help her friend.

"Arista!" the King called to her. "Come back at once!" But it was too late. Arista had almost reached the devilfish. Both she and Dylan were too close to the devilfish for Triton to try to stun it with his trident without hurting the young merpeople.

As Arista rode by the devilfish, she skimmed over its back with Tide. It whipped around to see who was bothering it now. It lashed its tail in Arista's direction, and its stinger rippled through the water. But Arista had already looped around out of its reach.

As soon as the devilfish had turned from him, Dylan rode to the side. Now it was his turn to distract the fish from Arista.

"Over here!" Dylan cried loudly, riding directly into the fish's path. The devilfish turned away from Arista and again took off after Dylan.

Dylan and Arista continued dizzying and confusing the devilfish with their expert riding. They took turns charging it and distracting it. As they did, they lured the deadly fish farther and farther away from the cove and from the others in the search party.

King Triton swam after his daughter and Dylan. He had his trident aimed in case the devilfish should strike again. When Dylan and Arista had lured the fish far out into the open sea, King Triton fired a bolt from his trident in the direction of the devilfish— close enough to scare it but not hurt it.

The devilfish, frightened, stopped pursuing Dylan and Arista and swam off.

"Safe," sighed the King. "Safe at last."

Dylan, Arista, and the King headed back to the search party, where everyone applauded vigorously.

"I've never seen such sea-horsemanship," said the Earl, complimenting Dylan and Arista.

"And the teamwork!" said Eddy. "I've never seen a girl ride so well. However did you learn?"

"Dylan taught her," Ariel explained. "Arista was always a good rider, but Dylan taught her about speed and precision."

"What?" King Triton bellowed, turning to

Ariel. "You knew about Dylan all along? Did you also know where Arista had gone tonight?"

"Well, I . . . ," sputtered Ariel.

"It's not her fault, Father," Arista spoke up. "I made her promise not to tell. It's true that Dylan taught me much of what I know. The teamwork you saw was the result of his coaching me, day after day. Sometimes we practiced when I was supposed to be at the royal parties."

"You could have been killed out there!" said the King.

"We saved Ariel's life," Arista tried to explain. "We never could have done that without all the hours of practice we've put in."

"Saved Ariel's life!" the King shouted. "Ariel wouldn't have been out here, trapped by a devilfish, in the first place if you'd been at the party as you should have been."

Arista turned to face the Earl and Eddy. "I'm sorry if you came all the way to the party for nothing," she said. "I truly am. But I couldn't abandon my friend."

The Earl smiled at her. "Oh, that's quite all right, my dear," he said. Then he turned to the King. "They do make an extraordinary team," he said, winking at Arista.

"Smashing!" agreed Eddy, clearly in awe.

"I would have been at the party tonight if Dylan could have come, too," Arista said, trying one last time to appeal to her father.

The King looked at his daughter. "Who *said* he *couldn't* come?" he asked angrily. The King had always prided himself on being fair and on being a good king to *all* his subjects. "I don't recall ever saying such a thing. I don't remember you ever asking for any invitation of the sort, Arista."

"Does that mean he *can* come?" Arista asked hopefully.

"Well," the King said, "I suppose Dylan could be our guest tomorrow night. As for tonight, the festivities are over. We've all had entirely too much excitement for one night."

10

The next night, the sisters gathered in the dressing room that adjoined their rooms. Once again they were getting ready for a party. Clothes were scattered everywhere. Adella was sitting at her dressing table, choosing one more time between her periwinkle tiara and her pearl one.

"What do you think?" she asked her sisters, trying on the tiara studded with pearls. "Should I switch back to the periwinkle?"

"NO!" her sisters shouted.

"Why do I feel like I've heard this before?" Andrina asked.

"Because you *have*," Alana said, giggling. "Last night and every other night since we got here!"

Arista swam in to join the others. All her sisters swarmed around her in a circle.

"So . . . is Dylan coming to the party tonight?" Adella asked.

Arista blushed. "Yes," she said, "he's coming. But I don't think Father is too thrilled about it."

"But he *did* invite him, right?" Ariel asked.

"Yes, but only for tonight," Arista said.

"Hey!" Alana cut her off. "I heard this Dylan is really cute!"

"Ooh!" all the sisters cooed, circling tighter around Arista. "And all the while you let us think you were off in the stables hanging around with sea horses!" Andrina said.

"I told you I wasn't afraid of boys," Arista said, laughing.

"Hey," Adella interrupted. She was now wearing her periwinkle tiara. "What do you think?" she asked. "Maybe I *should* switch back to the pearl one."

"NO!" her sisters chorused, collapsing in a fit of giggles.

As the sisters swam about the dressing room helping each other fasten their necklaces and straighten their jewels, Arista hurried to get dressed as well. When Arista and her sisters were ready—and Adella had changed to the pearl tiara and back to the periwinkle one more time—they swam down to the ballroom.

Dylan was waiting nervously for Arista at the entrance. He felt a little awkward but was excited just the same. He was also happy to see Arista. She looked very pretty.

Someone was at Dylan's side. It was Eddy. He smiled at the mermaids.

"Halloo!" Eddy called brightly. "Smashing news! As it turns out, I'm to escort one of you princesses after all. It's to be Ariel this time." Ariel looked around, trapped. "King's orders," Eddy insisted.

Ariel tried to muster a polite smile as Eddy took her arm and pulled her into the ballroom.

As the sisters glided into the ballroom, Sebastian raised his baton. But before he began, King Triton got up from his throne and asked for silence.

"I'd like to take a moment to acknowledge someone special tonight," said the King. "His name is Dylan. He behaved quite bravely yesterday, as did my daughter Arista."

Arista couldn't believe her ears. Was she dreaming? Her father, the King, was acknowledging her and Dylan right in front of everyone!

"I suppose by now," the King continued, "you've all heard about their escapade. I'd like to take this moment to welcome Dylan to our summer circle."

Applause broke out throughout the ballroom. As quickly as King Triton had gotten up to make the announcement, he took his place back on the throne. The ruler of the ocean was not one for long, gushy speeches. But Arista was touched just the same. She knew that her father's speech meant that he had accepted her friendship with Dylan.

When the applause died down, Sebastian struck up the band.

Everyone began to dance, including Arista

and Dylan. Eddy pulled Ariel onto the dance floor. "By Jove!" he exclaimed as he awkwardly led Ariel next to Arista and Dylan. "I think I've got the hang of this dancing business! And how are you faring, Ariel?"

In the most upper-crust accent she could muster, Ariel smiled at Eddy and said, "Swimmingly, my good fellow! Just swimmingly!"

Arista and Ariel exchanged a look over their dance partners' shoulders and burst into gales of laughter.